Mission Ziffoid

Michael Rosen

illustrated by **Arthur Robins**

WALKER BOOKS
AND SUBSIDIARIES
LONDON • BOSTON • SYDNEY

"Guess what? My brother's got a spaceship
with four mega-blast booster rockets."

"Wow! That's good."

"No, that's bad. On the way to Mars, the spaceship exploded into a million bits."

"Gosh! That's bad."

"No, he escaped
in his ejector seat."

"That's good."

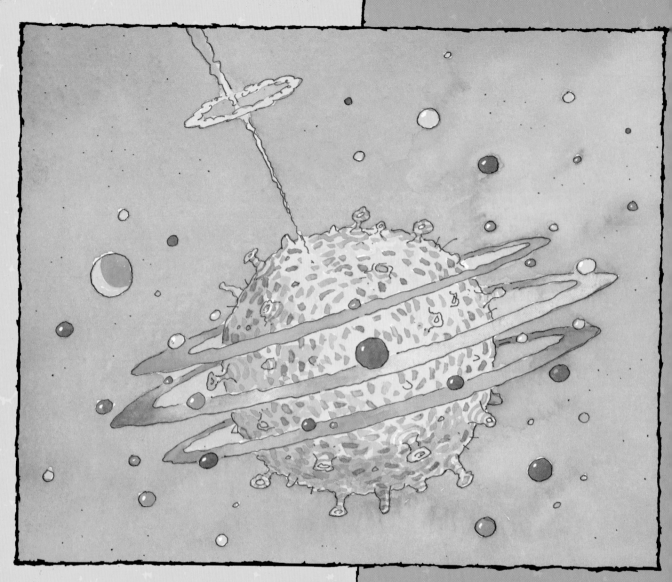

"No! That's bad. He crash-
landed on Ziffoid, a weird
planet zillions of miles away."

"Wow! That's bad."

"No, he landed on
some lovely soft stuff
and wasn't hurt at all."

"That's good."

"No! That's bad.
The lovely soft stuff
was a family of aliens."

"Ugh! That's bad."

"Oh no, that's good. The aliens thought he'd come to play football with them."

"That's good."

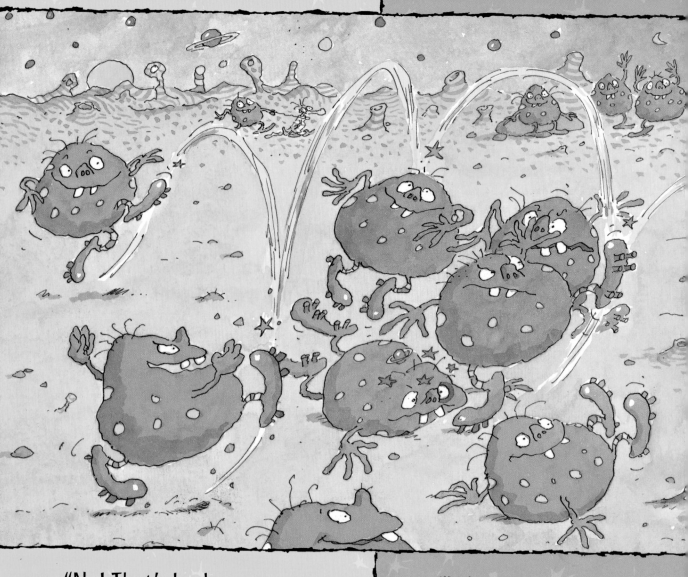

"No! That's bad.
My brother was the ball."

"Yikes! That *is* bad."

"No! That's good...

They kicked him into
their spaceship."

"Is that good?"

"No, that's bad. The aliens followed him inside."

"Oh, that's bad."

"No, that's good.
They said he could use
their spaceship to fly home."

"That *is* good."

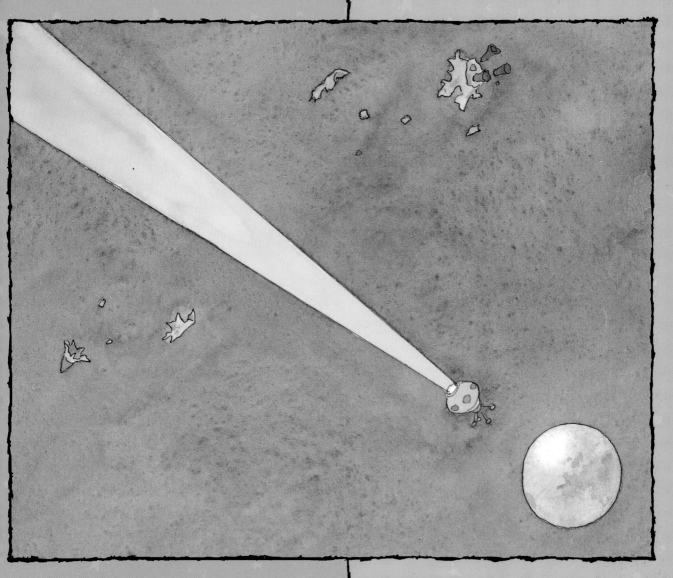

"No, no, no! That is *bad*."   **"Why?"**

First published 1999 by Walker Books Ltd, 87 Vauxhall Walk, London SE11 5HJ

2 4 6 8 10 9 7 5 3 1

Text © 1999 Michael Rosen   Illustrations © 1999 Arthur Robins

This book has been typeset in Myriad Tilt.
Printed in Hong Kong

British Library Cataloguing in Publication Data
A catalogue record for this book is available from the British Library.

ISBN 0-7445-5524-8